Bot Maker

# BUILD YOUR OWN SCRIBBLE BOT

Tucker Besel

BLACK RABBIT BOOKS

Hi Jinx is published by Black Rabbit Books
P.O. Box 3263, Mankato, Minnesota, 56002.
www.blackrabbitbooks.com


Jennifer Besel, editor; Michael Sellner, designer;
Omay Ayres, photo researcher



Library of Congress Cataloging-in-Publication Data
Names: Besel, Tucker, author.
Title: Build your own scribble bot / by Tucker Besel.
Description: Mankato, Minnesota : Black Rabbit Books, [2018] | Series: Hi jinx. Bot maker | Audience: Age 9-12. | Audience: Grade 4 to 6. | Includes bibliographical references and index.
Identifiers: LCCN 2017009988 (print) | LCCN 2017037522 (ebook) | ISBN 9781680723540 (e-book) | ISBN 9781680723243 (library binding) | ISBN 9781680726480 (paperback)
Subjects: LCSH: Robots—Design and construction—Juvenile literature. | Writing materials and instruments—Design and construction—Juvenile literature.
Classification: LCC TJ211.2 (ebook) | LCC TJ211.2 .B4843 2018 (print) | DDC 629.8/933—dc23
LC record available at https://lccn.loc.gov/2017009988

Printed in the United States. 7/18

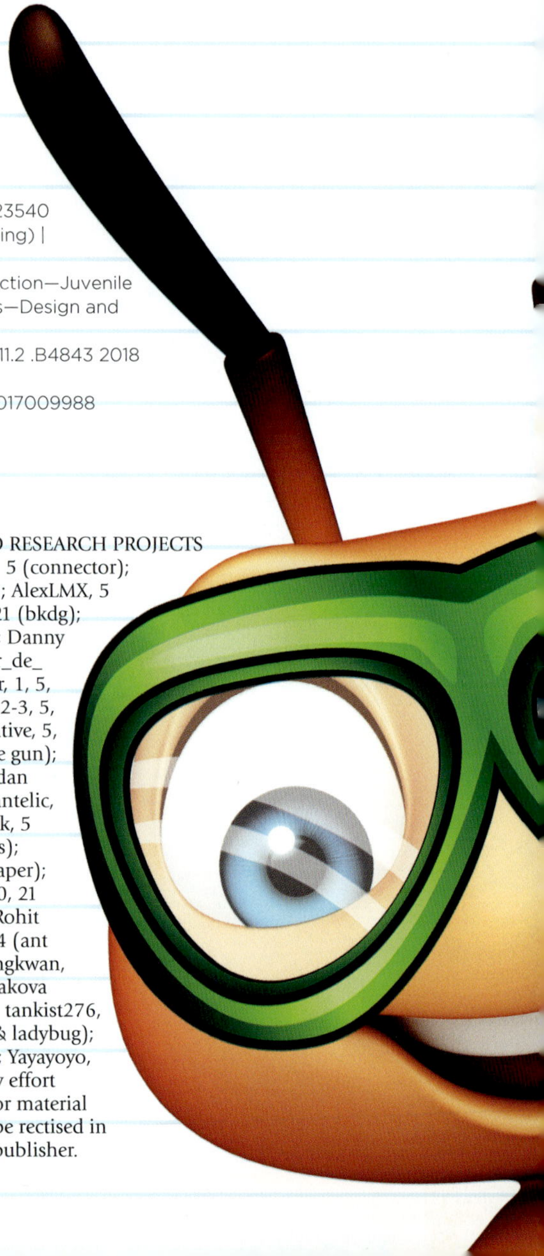

## Image Credits

Grant Gould, all robot illustrations
http://www.darpa.mil/: DEFENSE ADVANCED RESEARCH PROJECTS AGENCY, 20 (l); Shutterstock: 7th Son Studio, 5 (connector); advent, 4, 13 (kid); Alexandra Dzh, 16 (paint); AlexLMX, 5 (battery); Arcady, 17 (note); Art'nLera, 3, 12, 21 (bkdg); Besjunior, 10, 21 (farmer); Bplanet, 5 (motor); Danny Smythe, 5 (cup); Dualororua, 12 (arms); Fleur_de_papier, 18 (tape); Galyna G, Cover, Back Cover, 1, 5, 7, 8, 11, 15, 18-19 (bkgd); GraphicsRF, Cover, 2-3, 5, 19, 22 (goggles & paper clip); GreenStockCreative, 5, 15 (eraser); hoomoo, 9 (pliers); iceink, 5 (glue gun); Ilya Chalyuk, 3, 4, 6, 20 (marker stroke); Jourdan Laik, 5 (marker); Jumnong, 5 (tape); Mario Pantelic, 1 (scribbles); nikkytok, 5 (markers); Nosopyrik, 5 (ruler); opicobello, Cover, 1, 8 (marker strokes); Pasko Maksim, Back Cover, 10, 23, 24 (torn paper); Pitju, 3, 12, 21 (curled paper); Real Illusion, 10, 21 (overalls); Refluo, Cover, 18, 22 (mosquito); Rohit Dhanaji Shinde, Cover, 2–3 , 11, 16, 19, 22, 24 (ant & bee); S K Chavan, 18 (cone); Sarawut Padungkwan, Cover, 16, 19, 22 (ladybug & cockroach); Simakova Elena, 10 (grass); Sujono sujono, 6 (ladybug); tankist276, 5 (goggles); Teguh Mujiono, 6, 8, 15 (cricket & ladybug); totallypic, 6, 9, 10, 11, 12, 13, 14, 15 (arrows); Yayayoyo, 16 (brush); www.nasa.gov: NASA, 20 (r) Every effort has been made to contact copyright holders for material reproduced in this book. Any omissions will be rectised in subsequent printings if notice is given to the publisher.

# CONTENTS

# Chapter 1
# BE A BOT MAKER

Robots aren't just for TV shows. People are creating robots that run, battle, and do work. Even beginners can create bots that squiggle.

This book will help you make your own simple scribble robot. Robot building takes patience. Don't give up if something isn't working. Experiment until it does. And, most importantly, have fun!

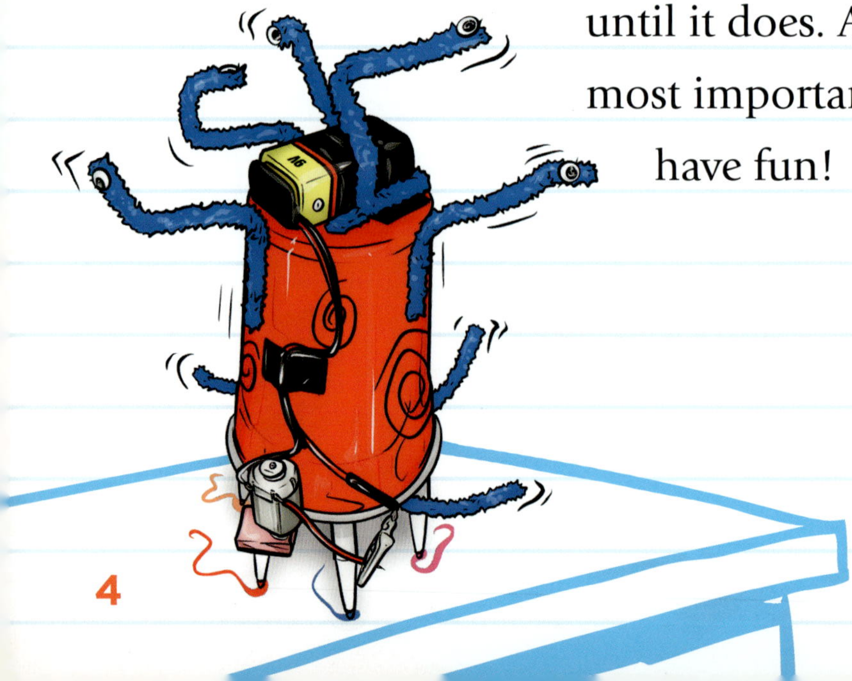

# WHAT YOU'LL NEED

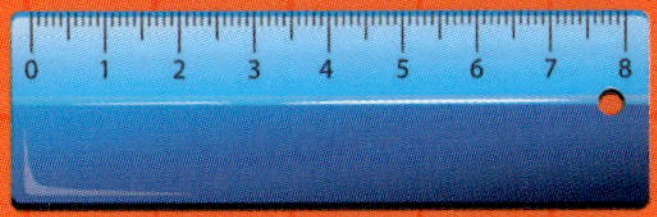
ruler

sharpened pencil

permanent marker

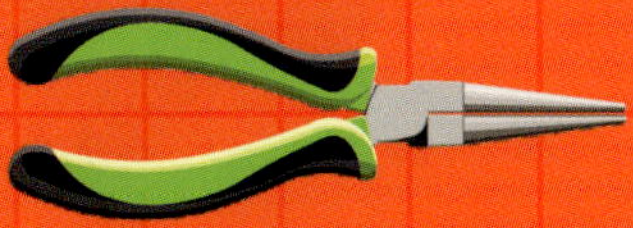
pliers

scissors

1¼-inch (3-cm) alligator clip

large eraser

googly eyes

pipe cleaners

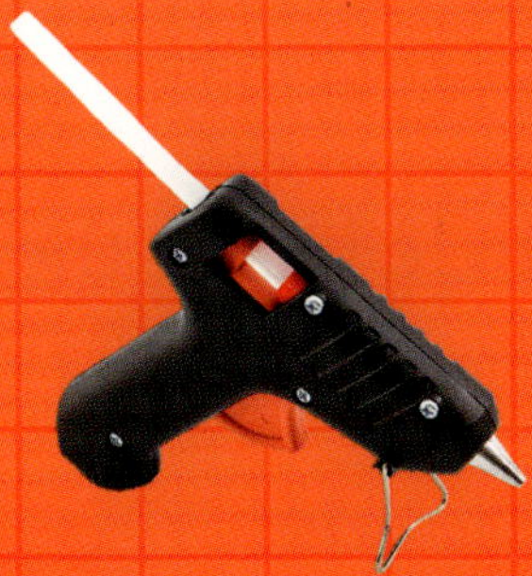
hot glue gun and hot glue

1 medium-large plastic cup

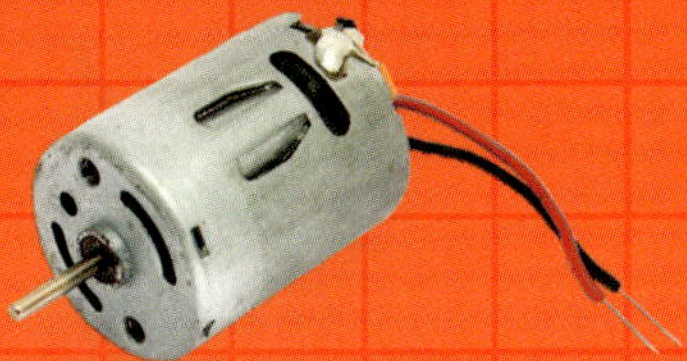
6-volt toy motor with wires (with ½ inch [1 cm] of wire exposed)

electrical tape

safety glasses

9-volt battery

9-volt battery snap connector (with ½ inch [1 cm] of wire exposed)

6 thin markers

Chapter 2

# LET'S BUILD!

**1.** Draw a circle inside the cup. It should be 2 inches (5 cm) from the bottom.

2. Tape three markers to the inside of the cup. Line up the bottoms of the markers with the circle you drew. Space the markers evenly around the cup.

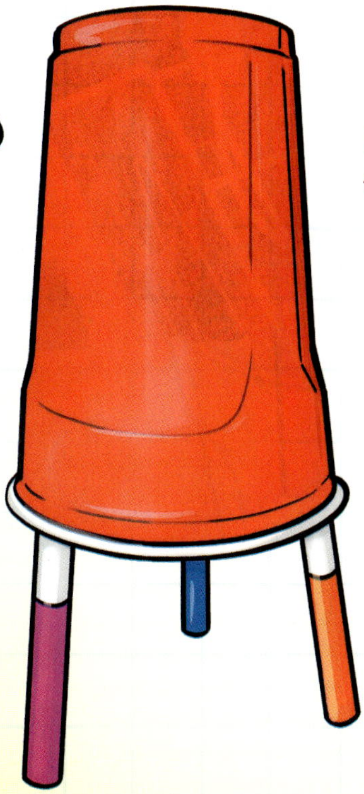

3. Flip the cup upside down. The markers should hold the cup up at an even height. If needed, adjust the markers. Then **secure** them in place with more tape.

4. Flip the cup over again. Tape the rest of the markers around the cup. Space them as evenly as possible. When you flip the cup over, the markers should touch the surface. The cup should be level too.

5. Attach the alligator clip to the motor's red wire. To do this, put the wire between the clip's tabs. Then use pliers to pinch the tabs together.

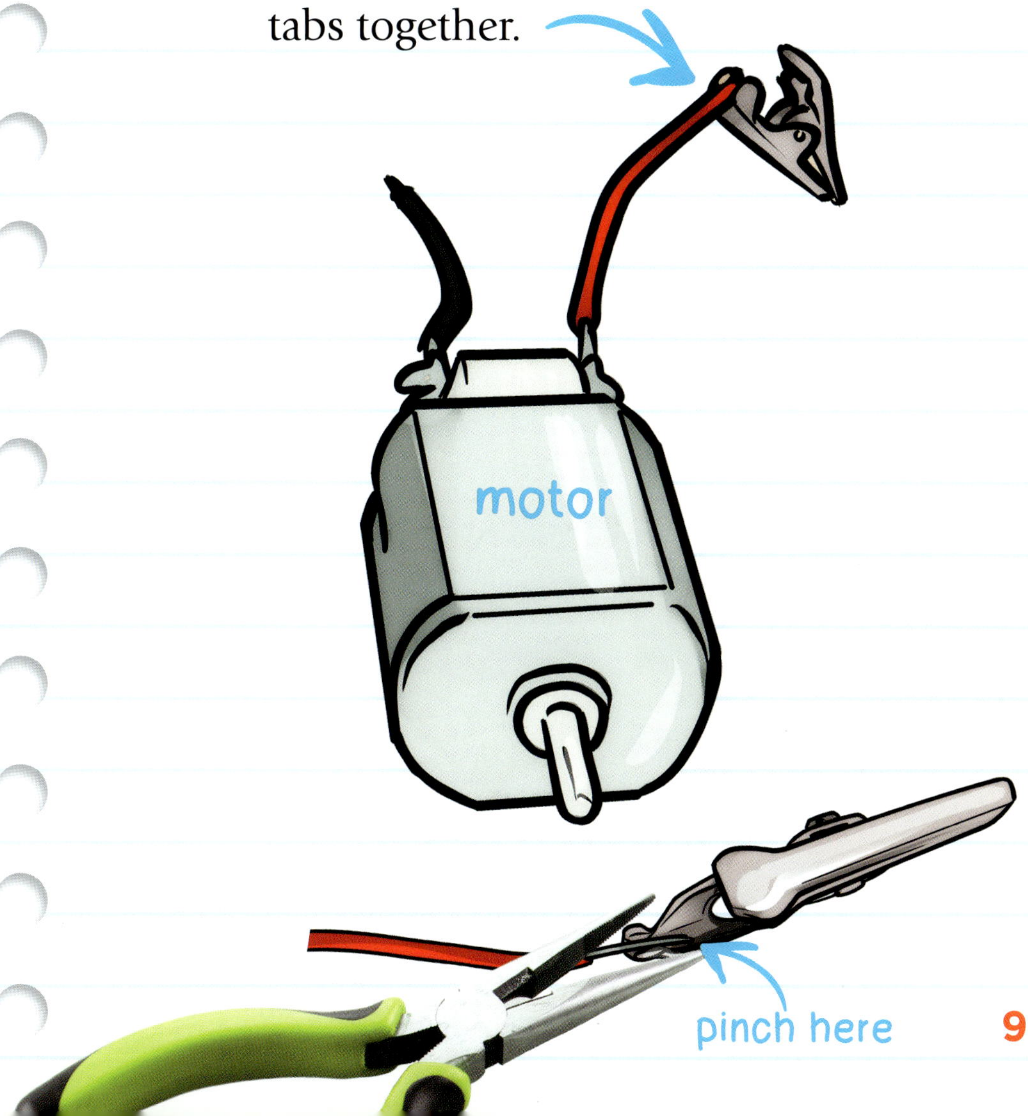

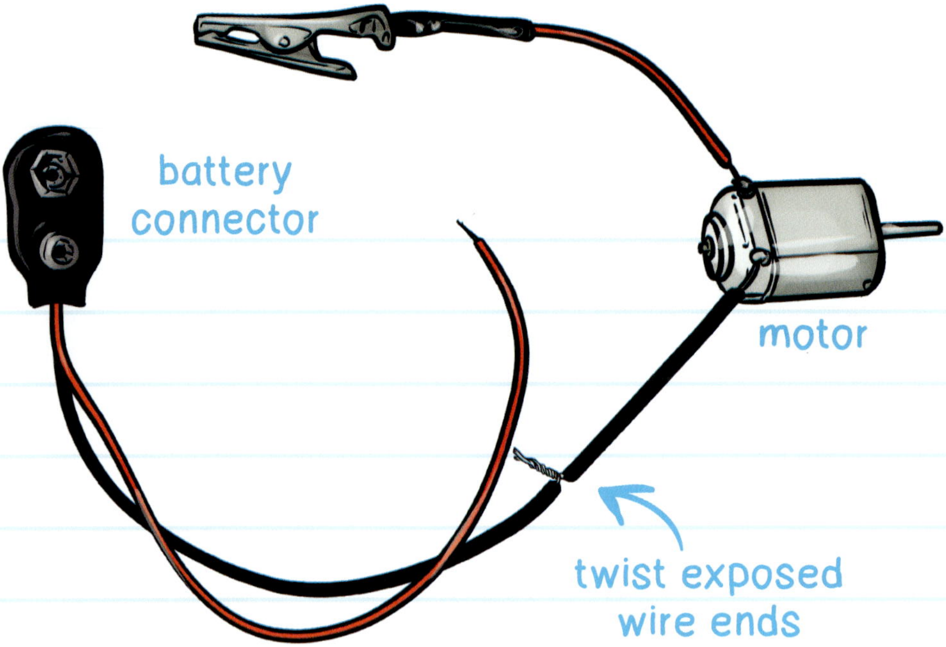


**6.** Connect the black wires from the battery connector and the motor. Hold the exposed wire ends side by side. Then twist them together.

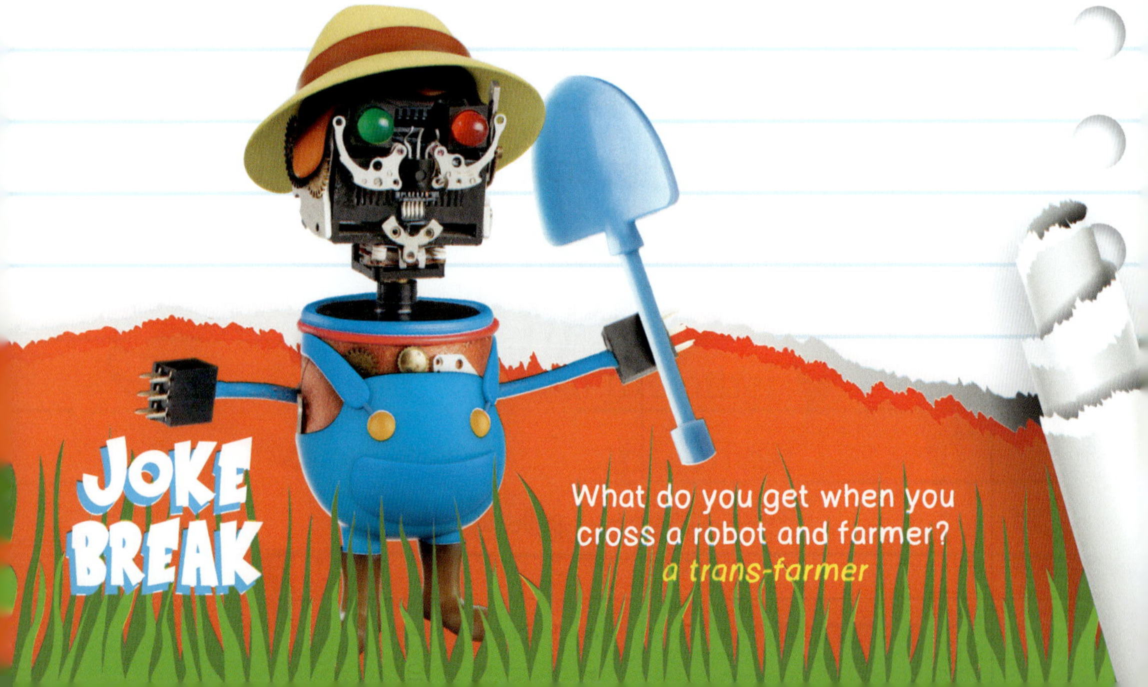

**JOKE BREAK**

What do you get when you cross a robot and farmer?

*a trans-farmer*

**7.** Snap a battery into the connector.

**8.** **Clamp** the alligator clip to the connector's exposed red wire. The motor's **shaft** should spin. Unclamp the clip.

9. Bend the twisted wire ends down. Wrap them to the black wire with electrical tape.

10. Tape the battery to the cup's bottom.

**11.** Hot glue the motor to the cup's lip below the battery. The shaft needs to stick out past the cup.

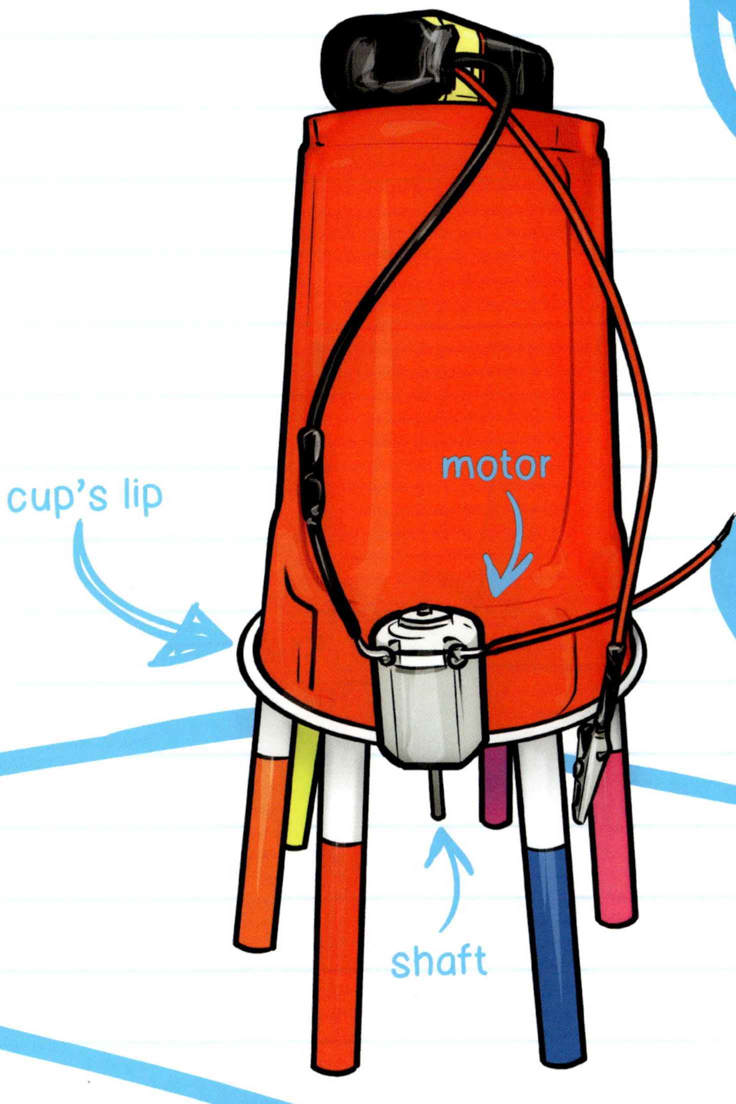

12. Clean up the wires. Fold them together, and tape them to the cup. Make sure the alligator clip can reach the exposed red wire.

**13.** Cut a 1 x ½-inch (2.5 x 1-cm) piece from the eraser.

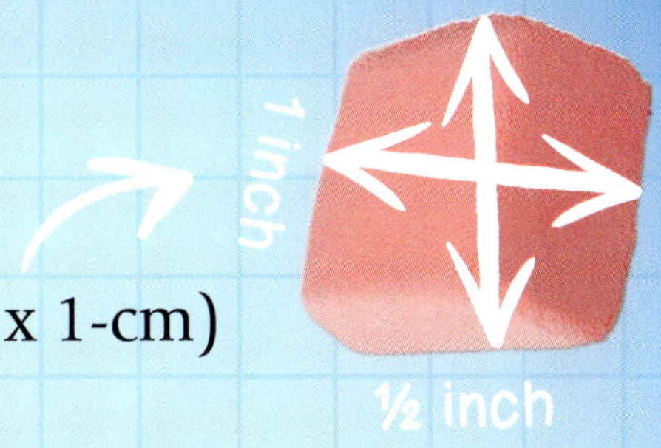

**14.** Use a pencil to poke a hole in the eraser. The hole should be a little off-center.

**15.** Press the motor's shaft into the eraser's hole. Hot glue the eraser to the shaft.

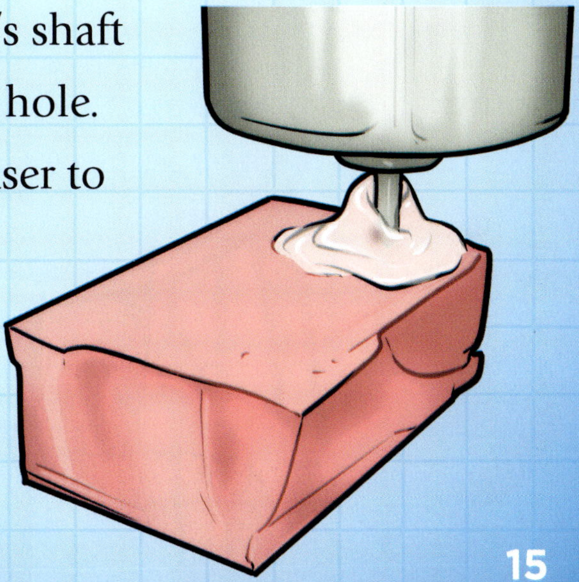

**16.** Decorate your scribble bot however you like. Maybe draw patterns on the cup. Glue pipe cleaners, googly eyes, or paper designs to the cup. Make the robot **represent** you.

Some robots look like real people. You could tape a photo of yourself to your bot. But, unless you have markers for legs, you won't fool anyone.

**17.** Now make your bot scribble! Lay a large piece of paper on your workspace. Take the caps off the makers. Clamp the alligator clip to the exposed red wire. You should feel the bot **vibrating**. Set the robot on the paper, and watch the cool patterns form! Be sure to have lots of space for the robot to scribble. Its path can be **unpredictable**.

**CAUTION CAUTION CAUTION**

If the eraser isn't glued on well, it could fly off. Wear safety glasses when the motor is spinning.

Chapter 3

# GET IN ON THE HI JINX

Robot scientists are doing amazing things. Robots help astronauts in space. Animal robots help soldiers in battle. Now you have basic robot-building skills. How will you change the world?

# Take It One Step More

1. What happens if you change the number of markers?

2. What could you use instead of a plastic cup?

3. How could you build on this design? Is there a way to make this robot start and stop on its own?

# GLOSSARY

**clamp** (KLAMP)—to hold tightly

**exposed** (ek-SPOZD)—not covered

**represent** (reh-pree-ZENT)—to serve as a sign or symbol of something

**secure** (suh-KEYR)—to hold fast

**shaft** (SHAFT)—a cylindrical bar used to support rotating pieces

**unpredictable** (un-pree-DIK-tuh-buhl)—not able to be known in advance

**vibrate** (VI-brayt)—to swing or move to and fro

# LEARN MORE

## BOOKS

**Cunningham, Kevin.** *Robot Scientist.* Cool STEAM Careers. Ann Arbor, MI: Cherry Lake Publishing, 2016.

**Derrington, Louise.** *How to Build Robots.* Technology in Motion. New York: Crabtree Publishing Company, 2017.

**McCombs, Kevin.** *Locomotion and Mechanics.* Robotics. New York: Cavendish Square Publishing, 2017.

## WEBSITES

Build Your First Robot
**www.popularmechanics.com/technology/robots/a7388/build-your-first-robot/**

History of Robotics: Timeline
**www.robotshop.com/media/files/PDF/timeline.pdf**

Robotics: Facts
**idahoptv.org/sciencetrek/topics/robots/facts.cfm**

# TIPS AND TRICKS

Adults are boring. But they can be really helpful. Don't be afraid to ask for help if you get stuck.

If your wires don't have exposed ends, don't worry. Use a wire stripper to take off as much of the wire casing as needed. (See the first tip.)

Try using different sizes of eraser to see which one works best. You could also try using a different material, such as cork.

The author is super cool. He made a short video of his scribble bot. Check it out on Black Rabbit Books' YouTube channel.